For all the great kids learning that making the best choices takes courage.

For Paula and Walter, with remembrance and love.
L.S.G.

For Madelyn, who is just sprouting her wings.
P.B.

NATIONAL LIBRARY OF CANADA CATALOGUING IN PUBLICATION DATA

Grossman, Linda Sky
Charlene's choice

(I'm a great little kid series)
Published in conjunction with Toronto Child Abuse Centre.
ISBN 1-896764-53-3 (bound).—ISBN 1-896764-47-9 (pbk.)

I. Self-esteem—Juvenile fiction. I. Bockus, Petra II. Toronto Child Abuse Centre. III. Title.
IV. Series: Grossman, Linda Sky. I'm a great little kid series.

PS8563.R65C46 2001   jC813'.6   C2001-902230-1
PZ7.G9084Ch 2001

Cover design: Stephanie Martin
Text design: Counterpunch/Peter Ross
Printed in Hong Kong, China

Toronto Child Abuse Centre gratefully acknowledges the support of the Ontario Trillium Foundation,
which provided funding for the I'm A Great Little Kid project. Further funding was generously provided by
TD Securities.

Second Story Press gratefully acknowledges the assistance of the Ontario Arts Council and the Canada Council
for the Arts for our publishing program. We acknowledge the financial support of the Government of Canada
through the Book Publishing Industry Development Program.

Published by
Second Story Press
720 Bathurst Street, Suite 301
Toronto, ON
M5S 2R4
www.secondstorypress.on.ca

Charlene's Choice

By Linda Sky Grossman

Illustrated by Petra Bockus

Second Story Press

Hi everyone, my name's Charlene,

I'm not short or tall, just in between.

I don't think you know me, or maybe you do,

But I have a problem, I'd like to tell it to you.

So here it is, the situation

That's causing me so much frustration.

Our science activity the other day

Was to discover how butterflies work and play.

Mr. Russell told us what we had to do,
And suggested we join in teams of two.
Sam and I decided to work together,
We'd done it before,

    when we learned about weather.

At the school library, Sam and I

Looked through the books with a careful eye.

We found great books that seemed just right,

And we each borrowed one for overnight.

Sam's book was even better than mine,

The butterflies' wings popped up, so fine.

The colors made us want to touch and feel,

Just to see if they might be real!

I returned my book almost right away,

But Sam said he needed his for another day.

Another day became one day more,

And before he knew it, he had passed day four!

Finally he said he wasn't giving it back,

Since the library had lots of copies on the rack.

"I'm keeping the book," he said with a grin,

"Tell if you want, but I won't give in!"

I knew for sure that this wasn't right,

But if I told on him, we'd be in a fight!

"Please, Sam," I said, "don't cause a fuss,

Give the book back, it's for all of us!"

Dad says in everything that happens each day,

I have a choice in what to do or say.

I must think about what I will choose,

Do I clean my room or take a snooze?

I could pretend Sam doesn't have the book,

But what if he gets caught when they start to look?

Being truthful is best, don't you agree?

Though if I tattle on Sam, he'll be angry with me.

I didn't sleep very well last night,

But now that it's morning, I know what is right.

Mr. Russell, our teacher, will lend a hand,

I'll explain it to him, he'll understand.

"Mr. Russell, I don't know what to do,
You said we could always come to you."
"Charlene," he said, "Let's sit down and we'll see,
If your problem can be solved by talking with me."

Mr. Russell and I talked for quite a while,
Until he got up and said with a smile,
"Your butterfly project was done very well,
Many lessons were learned from this, I can tell!"

"I'm happy you talked about the problem you had,

I'm sorry it caused you to feel so sad.

By the way, I found this book on my table,

Let's ask Sam to return it, when he's able!"

I spotted Sam because his jacket's bright red.

I gave him a hug, then I stood back and said,

"Sam, just think, your birthday will soon be here,

And I know what I'm going to buy you this year!"

Making choices can often be difficult, you see,

You might have to choose between one, two or three.

What would you choose, my newfound friend?

How would you have this story end?

For Grown-ups

Making Choices

Decision-making is the ability to choose between different ways of doing something, considering the risks and consequences of each option. For children to learn to make healthy choices they need the opportunity to practice age-appropriate decision-making. Children develop confidence in their ability to make decisions when they know they can ask for help and support if the choices are difficult or confusing.

Parents can support their children to learn how to make positive choices:

Provide opportunities for choice: Give your children the chance to make age-appropriate decisions every day.

Express confidence in their ability: Let your children know that you have faith in their ability to make reasonable choices.

Consider others: Consider your children's feelings when you make decisions, and they will learn to consider others in their decision-making.

Respect the choices of others: Show children that you respect the choices of others by accepting their decisions, as long as no one's well-being is jeopardized.

Consider different points of view: Show children that you value what others say, but have the confidence to make decisions that are right for you.